NANA

NANA

by Lyn Littlefield Hoopes

Drawings by Arieh Zeldich

Harper & Row, Publishers

NANA

Text copyright © 1981 by Lyn Littlefield Hoopes
Illustrations copyright © 1981 by Arieh Zeldich
Printed in the United States of America. For information address Harper & Row, Publishers, Inc., 10 East 53rd Street, New York, N.Y. 10022. Published simultaneously in Canada by Fitzhenry & Whiteside Limited, Toronto.

Library of Congress Cataloging in Publication Data
Hoopes, Lyn Littlefield.
  Nana.

  Summary: Although her grandmother has died, a young girl still sees her in all the things living and growing around her.
  [1. Grandmothers—Fiction.   2. Death—Fiction]
I. Zeldich, Arieh, date.   II. Title.
PZ7.H7703Nan 1981   [E]   81-47110
ISBN 0-06-022574-2   AACR2
ISBN 0-06-022575-0 (lib. bdg.)

First Edition

To my mother,
for the understanding

NANA

I am at Nana's house,
but Nana is not here.
Her room is still as morning.
The window is open partway
for sleeping,
and the sun lines the curtains
like she is here,
but she is not.
Our Nana died in the night.

I sit on the stool by Nana's window.
Here are her slippers,
and here are her glasses
by the book on the table.
I think,
we will read a story,
but no,
we will not.

In the garden the bird feeder
swings with the wind.
No flowers grow now,
but in the shadow of old stalks
baby ferns
curl up through wet brown leaves.
If you are very quiet,
Nana says, you can hear them unfurl.

I listen.
And I think,
Nana went to bed,
just like every night.
Is she asleep now, I wonder.
Is it like that?
I try to remember:
What was it like before I was born?

I cannot tell.
And so I go out,
along the stone wall by Nana's window
and beyond, to the field.
The grass ripples gold like the sea.
In a hollow near the woods
the sun is warm.

I lie down and the breeze
ripples all around me.
I close my eyes.
The sun does an orange-and-yellow
flicker dance.
I am spinning light,
high-whirling, flickering, breeze light.
The ground is far away.
The wind and sun are far away too,
and still I am here.
Here and everywhere.
Always.
I am the me that was
me before I was born.

The sun in my face is warm.
I see Nana
on a silver summer morning.
The grass shines white with dew
and a bird hops for worms
outside her garden.
Nana comes near me
by the window and calls,
"Chick-a-dee,
chick-a-dee-dee-dee-dee-dee."
She touches her finger to my lips.
We are quiet,
and soon we hear our answer.
"Chick-a-dee-dee-dee, chick-a-dee."

I feel the breeze now,
and the ground
cool and damp beneath me.
Nana cannot hear the wind.
The sun does not touch her.
But she is here, beside me.

At the edge of the woods I hear a bird.
Low, in the rustling branches.
I step gently in on the soft moss.
Young fiddler ferns are pushing up
through wet brown leaves.
I stop, and listen.

"Chick-a-dee, chick-a-dee-dee-dee."
Where is the bird?
In the stump of a dead birch
someone is building a new nest.
I cannot see him,
but I know he is here.

I am quiet, listening.
The trees are still now too.
We are quiet together,
and then I hear a leaf rustle
and the whisper-hush
of a fern unfurling.

I wait,
and again I sing,
"Chick-a-dee,
chick-a-dee-dee-dee-dee-dee."
I watch and listen with the trees.
I am very still,
for I know he is near.
And Nana too
is here.